Brilliant

Brillante

Reading-Coloring-Word Search-Word Define-Journaling

ACKNOWLEDGEMENT

I Would Like To Acknowledge The
CREATOR OF HEAVEN AND EARTH
(GOD) FOR ALL THAT HE HAS Given
Me. Thanking God I Am For My
Talents and Gifts.
I Recognize That The Lord Gave Me
This Gift, Which Allows Me To
Share With Children And Everyone
That Participates In The Reading Of
The Literary Material That I
Produce Through The Commission
Of God.

Thank You
Lord God
I Will Forever Be Grateful
For Your Trust In Me

Pamela Denise Brown
Goodwill Ambassador
For The Positive Cultivation Of Children

My Collection Of EDUCATIONAL Books are designed to foster the social development of children psychologically. My books are designed to help children become psychologically sociable, culturally sensitive and aware so children can co-exist in diversity and become successful in life. I believe the books I write will transform the minds of children, which ultimately will cause them to pause, to think and make better choices.

My EDUCATIONAL Books are designed to effectuate change and influence success in the lives of every child.

The Smart Books in the Collection are Reinforcements to Learning.

My EDUCATIONAL books will help build children's self-esteem and confidence to a level that will help them socially engage in a diverse world with confidence and harmony and ultimately prepare them for life

Books Speak For You books may be ordered through booksellers or by contacting:
Booksspeakforyou.com
The views expressed in this work are solely those of the author.
Any illustration provided by iStock and such images are being used for illustrative purposes.
Certain stock imagery © iStock.
ISBN: 978-1-64050-357-1
Library of Congress Control No: 2018908350
Printed in the United States Of America

Brilliant

Brillante

Reading-Coloring-Word Search-Word Define-Journaling

Brilliant Is What I Look At When I Look At Me

ESPAÑOL
Brillante es lo que miro cuando me miro

Brilliant Is What I Am
In Everything I Desire To Be

ESPAÑOL
Brillante es lo que soy en todo lo
que deseo ser

Brilliance Is What I
Demonstrate
When I Walk Out The Door

ESPAÑOL
El brillo es lo que demuestro
cuando salgo de la puerta

Brilliance Is What My
Teachers See
When I Hit The Classroom Floor

ESPAÑOL
El brillo es lo que mi
Los maestros ven
Cuando llegué al piso del aula

Brilliant Is What
I'm Taught To Be
In All My Creativity

ESPAÑOL
Brillante es lo que me enseñaron a
estar en toda mi creatividad

Brilliant Is What I Want You To Say When You Identify Me

ESPAÑOL
Brillante es lo que quiero que digas
cuando me identifiques

Brilliant Is What I've Worked
So Hard Every Day
To Achieve

ESPAÑOL
Brillante es lo que he trabajado tan
duro todos los días para lograr

Brilliant Is
My Payoff
To Me Being Me

ESPAÑOL
Brillante es mi recompensa
Para mí ser yo

COLOR ME

COLOR ME

Brilliant Definition

bril·liant

adjective

adjective: **brilliant**

1.

exceptionally clever or talented.
"a brilliant young mathematician"

synonyms:	bright, intelligent, clever, smart, astute, intellectual; More
antonyms:	stupid

   • outstanding; impressive.
"his brilliant career at Harvard"

synonyms:	superb, glorious, illustrious, impressive, remarkable, exceptional
	"his brilliant career"
antonyms:	unremarkable

   • BRITISH*informal*
very good, excellent, or marvelous.
"we had a brilliant time"

WORD SEARCH

SEARCH AND FIND

BRILLIANT 3 TIMES

BRIGHT 3 TIMES

CLEVER 3 TIMES

SMART 3 TIMES

ASTUTE 3 TIMES

OUTSTANDING

INTELLECT

IMPRESSIVE

GLORIOUS

REMARKABLE

EXCEPTIONAL

B	R	I	L	L	I	A	N	T	S	V
R	C	L	E	V	E	R	Y	P	M	X
E	X	C	E	P	T	I	O	N	A	L
M	S	M	A	R	T	K	V	O	R	S
A	I	M	P	R	E	S	S	Q	T	W
R	F	T	X	M	B	R	I	G	H	T
K	V	B	R	I	L	L	I	A	N	T
A	G	L	O	R	I	O	U	S	H	J
B	S	U	P	E	R	B	K	T	L	R
I	B	R	I	G	H	T	V	U	E	P
E	R	E	V	E	L	C	U	T	O	Z
A	S	T	U	T	E	T	R	E	C	M
I	N	T	E	L	L	E	C	T	I	O
I	M	P	R	E	S	S	I	V	E	N
B	R	I	L	L	I	A	N	T	V	K
U	N	R	E	M	F	R	K	N	E	T
T	S	M	A	R	T	H	G	I	Y	B
I	M	P	R	E	Q	A	N	O	Z	Y
O	U	T	S	T	A	N	D	I	N	G

WORD DEFINE

LOOK UP THE MEANING OF THESE 3 WORDS AND WRITE THEM IN A SENTENCE

1. Smart_____

_____

_____

_____

_____

_____

_____

_____

_____

_____

_____

_____

_____

_____

2. Bright_____

_____

_____

_____

_____

_____

_____

_____

_____

_____

_____

_____

_____

_____

_____

_____

_____

_____

_____

_____

3. Exceptional_____

_____

_____

_____

_____

_____

_____

_____

_____

_____

_____

_____

_____

_____

_____

_____

_____

_____

_____

Journaling

Write Down What You Want To Be And
How You Plan On Becoming It

_____

_____

_____

_____

_____

_____

_____

_____

_____

_____

_____

_____

_____

_____

A Special Dedication With Love To ALL THE CHILDREN In COUNTRIES AROUND THE WORLD

- A

- Afghanistan
- Albania
- Algeria
- Andorra
- Angola
- Antigua and Barbuda
- Argentina
- Armenia
- Australia
- Austria
- Azerbaijan
- B
- Bahamas
- Bahrain
- Bangladesh
- Barbados
- Belarus
- Belgium
- Belize
- Benin
- Bhutan
- Bolivia
- Bosnia and Hiszegovina
- Botswana
- Brazil
- Brunei
- Bulgaria
- Burkina Faso
- Burundi
- C
- Cabo Verde
- Cambodia
- Cameroon
- Canada
- Central African Republic (CAR)
- Chad
- Chile
- China
- Colombia
- Comoros
- Democratic Republic of the Congo
- Republic of the Congo
- Costa Rica
- Cote d'Ivoire
- Croatia
- Cuba
- Cyprus
- Czech Republic
- D
- Denmark
- Djibouti

- Dominica
- Dominican Republic
- E
- Ecuador
- Egypt
- El Salvador
- Equatorial Guinea
- Eritrea
- Estonia
- Ethiopia
- F
- Fiji
- Finland
- France
- G
- Gabon
- Gambia
- Georgia
- Germany
- Ghana
- Greece
- Grenada
- Guatemala
- Guinea
- Guinea-Bissau
- Guyana
- H
- Haiti
- Honduras
- Hungary
- I
- Iceland
- India
- Indonesia
- Iran
- Iraq
- Ireland
- Israel
- Italy
- J
- Jamaica
- Japan
- Jordan
- K
- Kazakhstan
- Kenya
- Kiribati
- Kosovo
- Kuwait
- Kyrgyzstan
- L
- Laos
- Latvia
- Lebanon
- Lesotho

- Liberia
- Libya
- Liechtenstein
- Lithuania
- Luxembourg
- M
- Macedonia
- Madagascar
- Malawi
- Malaysia
- Maldives
- Mali
- Malta
- Marshall Islands
- Mauritania
- Mauritius
- Mexico
- Micronesia
- Moldova
- Monaco
- Mongolia
- Montenegro
- Morocco
- Mozambique
- Myanmar (Burma)
- N
- Namibia
- Nauru
- Nepal
- Nethislands
- New Zealand
- Nicaragua
- Niger
- Nigeria
- North Korea
- Norway
- O
- Oman
- P
- Pakistan
- Palau
- Palestine
- Panama
- Papua New Guinea
- Paraguay
- Peru
- Philippines
- Poland
- Portugal

- Q
- Qatar
- R
- Romania
- Russia

- Rwanda
- S
- St. Kitts and Nevis
- St. Lucia
- St. Vincent and the Grenadines
- Samoa
- San Marino
- Sao Tome and Principe
- Saudi Arabia
- Senegal
- Serbia
- Seychelles
- Sierra Leone
- Singapore
- Slovakia
- Slovenia
- Solomon Islands
- Somalia
- South Africa
- South Korea
- South Sudan
- Spain
- Sri Lanka
- Sudan
- Suriname
- Swaziland
- Sweden
- Switzerland
- Syria
- T
- Taiwan
- Tajikistan
- Tanzania
- Thailand
- Timor-Leste
- Togo
- Tonga
- Trinidad and Tobago
- Tunisia
- Turkey
- Turkmenistan
- Tuvalu
- U
- Uganda
- Ukraine
- United Arab Emirates (UAE)
- United Kingdom (UK)
- United States of America (USA)
- Uruguay

- Uzbekistan
- V
- Vanuatu
- Vatican City (Holy See)
- Venezuela
- Vietnam
- Y
- Yemen
- Z
- Zambia
- Zimbabwe

ANOTHER SPECIAL DEDICATION TO
ALL THE CHILDREN WITH LOVE
IN CITIES IN THE
UNITED STATES OF AMERICA
Find Your City

And

Highlight It

Albuquerque, NM
Anchorage, AK
Albany, NY
Annapolis, MD

Atlanta, GA

Corpus Christi, TX

Atlantic City, NJ

Dallas, TX

Augusta, ME

Davenport, IA

Austin, TX

Daytona, FL

Bakersfield, CA

Denver, CO

Baltimore, MD

Des Moines, IA

Baton Rouge, LA

Des Plaines, IL

Billings, MT

Detroit, MI

Biloxi, MS

Dover, DE

Bismarck, ND

Durham, NC

Bloomsburg, PA

Erie, PA

Boise, ID

Eugene, OR

Boston, MA

Fayetteville, NC

Buffalo, NY

Flagstaff, AZ

Burlington, VT

Frankfort, KY

Carson City, NV

Ft. Lauderdale, FL

Charleston, SC

Gettysburg, PA

Charleston, WV

Greenville, SC

Charlotte, NC

Hampton Roads, VA

Charlottesville, VA

Harrisburg, PA

Cheyenne, WY

Hartford, CThroough

Chicago, IL

Chicago, IL

Helena, MT

Cleveland, OH

Hollywood, CA

Colorado Springs, CO

Honolulu, HI

Columbia, SC

Houston, TX

Columbus, OH

Huntsville, AL

Concord, CA

Indianapolis, IN

Concord, NH

Jackson, MS

Jackson Hole-Grand
Tetons, WY
Jacksonville, FL
Jefferson City, MO
Jim Thorpe, PA
Juneau, AK
Kansas City, MO
Knoxville, TN
Lake Tahoe, NV
Lancaster, PA
Lancaster / Central
PA
Lansing, MI
Las Vegas, NV
Las Vegas, NV
Lexington, KY
Lincoln, NE
Little Rock, AR
Long Island, NY
Los Angeles, CA
Los Angeles, CA
Louisville, KY
Madison, WI
Manchester, NH
Maryville, TN
Memphis, TN
Miami, FL
Miami, FL
Milwaukee, WI

Minneapolis, MN
Mobile, AL
Montgomery, AL
Montpelier, VT
Morrison, IL
Nashville, TN
New Haven, CT
New Orleans, LA
New York: Bronx
New York: Brooklyn
New York:
Manhattan
New York: Queens
New York City
Newark, NJ
Niagara Falls, NY
Northville, MI
Oklahoma City, OK
Orlando, FL
Olympia, WA
Omaha, NE
Orange County, CA
Palm Springs, CA
Pensacola, FL
Philadelphia, PA
Phoenix, AZ
Pierre, SD
Pittsburgh, PA
Portland, ME

Portland, OR
Providence, RI
Pueblo, CO
Raleigh, NC
Rapid City, SD
Reno, NV
Richmond, VA
Sacramento, CA
Salt Lake City, UT
San Diego, CA
San Francisco, CA
Santa Cruz, CA
Santa Fe, NM
Scranton, PA
Seattle, WA
Sedona, AZ
Shreveport, LA
Silicon Valley, CA
Springfield, IL
St. Joseph, MO

St. Paul, MN
St. Louis, MO
State College, PA
SurfScranton, PA
Syracuse, NY
Tacoma, WA
Tallahassee, FL
Tampa, FL
Topeka, KS
Trenton, NJ
Tulsa, OK
Tuscon, AZ
Tyler, TX
Washington, DC
Wichita, KS
Wilkes-Barre, PA
Williamsburg, VA
Williamsport, PA
Wilmington, DE
Yuma, AZ

Thank You

For Purchasing This Book
In Your Purchase, You Are Celebrating
With Me The Completion Of One Of
God's Many Works Through Me.

Pamela Denise Brown

Contact Information
Website:

Booksspeakforyou.com

1-800-757-0598

OR

267-318-8933

@Booksspeakforu (twitter)

Email:

Booksspeakforyou@yahoo.com

FaceBook @Booksspeakforyou

BOOKS SPEAK FOR YOU

www.ingramcontent.com/pod-product-compliance
Lightning Source LLC
Chambersburg PA
CBHW041030170626
46815CB00001B/40